BETTY'S WEDDING

WRITTEN AND ILLUSTRATED BY

MICHAEL BRAGG

MACMILLAN PUBLISHING COMPANY • NEW YORK

BETTY'S WEDDING

A photograph album of my
big sister's wedding.

An invitation
to the Wedding
of Elizabeth
and
James.

This is me with my younger
brother Henry who I have to
share a bedroom with.
I am going to be a bridesmaid
when my big sister Betty gets married.

This is a picture of Betty with Jim who is going to become her husband in June.

The newspaper announcement of the wedding.

Forthcoming Weddings

Mr. J. T. Powell and Miss E. M. Felix
The engagement is announced between James Thomas, son of Mr and Mrs D. C. Powell of Newport, and Elizabeth Mary, eldest daughter of Mr and Mrs A. J. Felix of Cambridge. The marriage will take place in June.

This is Betty with Mummy
and Daddy and Bear.
Mummy is not pleased
because Daddy wouldn't
change his suit.

Jim with his bicycle.
Henry likes the bicycle.

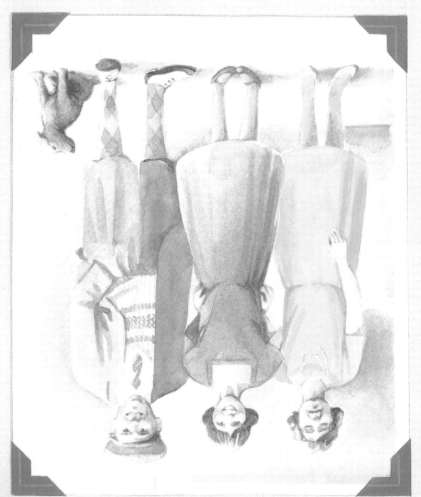

While the grown-ups look at old photographs we help finish up the left-overs.

This is us at Sunday lunch when lots of relatives and friends come to meet Jim and Betty and talk about the wedding.

Betty wouldn't hold my hand for this picture. She said it was still sticky from lunch.

Betty has found an old photograph of Daddy.

She thought the photographs were very funny until Henry found pictures of her as a baby.

Me and Henry and our cousin are going to help Auntie Gina make the wedding cake. Auntie sends Blazer out of the kitchen.

We take turns at stirring the mixture. This is when Henry lost a shirt button. At the end we are allowed to lick the spoons and bowls.

This is a sample of the fabric for my dress.

Betty's dress

Mummy and Betty choosing the material for the wedding dress.

We all go shopping to buy things Betty needs for the wedding and afterwards.

Hours later we are still shopping.

More hours later — the car is full of parcels and we are all tired. The shopping is finished.

At last we can have a Popsicle.

I have saved the sticks.

Now it's Henry's turn but he doesn't like being photographed in his pageboy suit. We had to hold his hands to keep him to keep still.

I am having a fitting for my dress but Henry is laughing at me. Bessie has found a pin.

Betty and Jim have received lots of presents. All the invitations have been sent and hundreds of people are coming. It is not long now to the wedding so we all have to have haircuts.

Henry's hair

Blazer's

A cutting from my hair.

Aunt Millie

Cousin Lisa who always cries.

It is the morning of the wedding and hundreds of flowers arrive. Then guests start arriving. Here are some of them ~

~ June ~

Elliott. Jim's best man who looks after the ring.

Aunt Mary with the hat that was too big.

Grandad.

Uncle Ivor who took some of the photographs.

Aunt Maud.

Cousin Claud.

It is nearly time to go and Uncle Stan takes a photograph of me in the garden in my dress. Roger has heard Betty shouting because she cannot find her shoes.

Some guests are still getting ready.

At last we're off. Some of the guests went to the church in an open top coach. Not everyone could agree on the best route to get there.

Henry thought he'd try to go on Jim's bicycle.

One car got stuck on the way to the church.

Betty and Daddy were last looking very grand in an old open top cadillac.

a piece of ribbon from the cars.

And some had difficulty getting out when they did get there.

Everyone is waiting.
Jim checks that Elliott
has the ring.

Blazer has to stay
in the car.

At last they arrive — towing
the car that broke down.

Betty and Daddy rush
in and we can start.

At last the wedding. Me and Henry stand right behind the couple where everyone can see us. Betty looks lovely. She wears the ring and they are married.

This is one I took.

When they left the church people threw confetti and lots of photographs were taken.

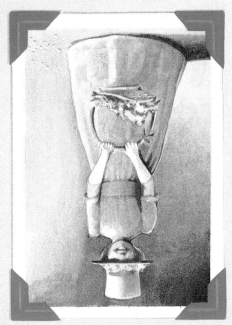

This is me in Jim's hat.

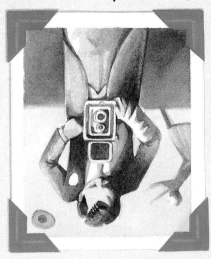

Uncle Jim again. Aunt Mary never did find her hat.

While people were taking photographs Aunt Mary's big hat blew away.

The bedroom I have to share with Henry.

We all went back to our house where there was an enormous tent in the garden for everyone to go in.

We all had lots to eat and Uncle Ivor did a trick with a sausage.

Then there was music and dancing and we joined in.

Guess what I found in my piece of cake?

Betty and Jim cut the cake together. Henry wanted a piece first and was told you don't do that at weddings.

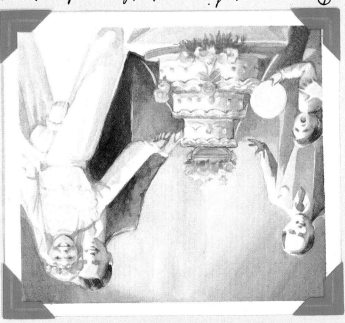

Betty and Jim have changed into different clothes and are going away on vacation. Everyone comes out to say goodbye. Elliott puts the suitcase in the car and discovers Henry hiding in the backseat.

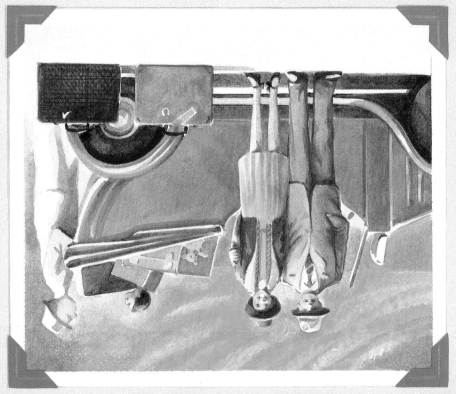

Betty promises to send me a postcard and just before they go Jim gives me a present for being such a good bridesmaid.

Here I am wearing my present — a wristwatch of my own.

At last they're off. Everyone waves. Somebody has tied lots of things to the back of the car and we find out where that big hat went.

The party carries on and all the grown ups act very silly. Henry has already gone to bed but I can stay up later. I feel a little sad because now I won't see Betty every day.

But Mummy whispers I can have Betty's bedroom now. I feel sleepy and Daddy carries me up to bed.

THE END

Macmillan Publishing Company, 866 Third Avenue, New York, NY 10022
First published in Great Britain in 1988 by Methuen Children's Books Ltd, London
First American Edition 1988.
Printed in Belgium by Henri Proost, Turnhout, Belgium.

10 9 8 7 6 5 4 3 2 1

The text of this book was hand-lettered.
The illustrations were rendered in watercolor,
gouache, Cryla and colored pencils on Hollingworth wash and Daler line board.
The endpapers were marbled by Compton Marbling, Tisbury, England.

Library of Congress Cataloging-in-Publication Data
Bragg, Michael.   Betty's wedding.
Summary: Through a series of captioned paintings of photographs from a family album,
a younger sister describes the events of her older sister's wedding day.
[1. Weddings—Fiction] I. Title. PZ7.B733Be 1988   [E]   87-34866
ISBN 0-02-711880-0